Your Auntie Loves You

Aimee Hall & Kimberly Brown

LifeRich Publishing is a registered trademark of The Reader's Digest Association, Inc.

LifeRich Publishing books may be ordered through booksellers or by contacting:

LifeRich Publishing
1663 Liberty Drive
Bloomington, IN 47403
www.liferichpublishing.com
1 (888) 238-8637

Because of the dynamic nature of the Internet, any web addresses or links contained in this book may have changed since publication and may no longer be valid. The views expressed in this work are solely those of the author and do not necessarily reflect the views of the publisher, and the publisher hereby disclaims any responsibility for them.

Any people depicted in stock imagery provided by Thinkstock are models, and such images are being used for illustrative purposes only.
Certain stock imagery © Thinkstock.

ISBN: 978-1-4897-1091-8 (sc)
ISBN: 978-1-4897-1090-1 (e)

Print information available on the last page.

LifeRich Publishing rev. date: 3/25/2017

Dedication:

To Ella Grace, my pretty girl, my little monkey. I never knew how much I could love someone so instantly until you entered into this world! The love for you is greater than imagined, I love being your 'Auntie Aimee' and I cannot wait to see what your adventures are before you.

To Brady, my handsome boy, my little tiger. Welcoming you into my life reassures me, my heart is big enough to truly love so much greater than I thought humanly possible. I love being your 'Auntie Aimee' and am excited to see you grow.

To all future nieces and/or nephews and all my honorary nieces and nephews being your AUNTIE is the best feeling ever and I am honored to have that place in your little lives.

- Auntie Aimee

To Koty, Dalton, Savannah, Wyatt, Cayden, Tait and Rylee. I am beyond blessed to be your Aunt Kimmy/ KiKi. Each one of you are so special to me and I love you so much and am so grateful that I get to make special memories with each of you. There are some pretty special ones! I truly feel like God gave me an important and the best job as an aunt! I love you!

- Aunt Kimmy/KiKi

About the Authors:

Aimee Hall was born and raised in a little town in Kentucky, which translates to a Kentucky Wildcat fan, especially during basketball season. When Aimee is not cheering on her Kentucky Wildcats she is working, spending time with her family (especially her niece and nephew), shopping or attending other sporting events. Aimee is a new author who never dreamed of writing a children's book until her niece was born and she couldn't find an Aunt(ie) book to read to her.

Kimberly Brown is a full time children's educator in Dallas, Texas. She is passionate about teaching children and being an aunt. In her free time she enjoys watching and attending sporting events, traveling, crafting, singing and shopping. She is a collector of many children's books and loves to read stories to children.

To:

From:

Your auntie loves you more today and
even more than yesterday.

Your auntie loves you because at first sight,
she loved you with all her might.

Your auntie loves you when you are sleeping,

And even when you are weeping.

Your auntie loves you when you are hungry,

And even when you are funny.

Your auntie loves you when you smile,

And will always go the extra mile.

Your auntie loves you when you are fresh and clean,

And even when we both scream.

Your auntie loves you when you wake her up at night,

And when you are up at first light.

Your auntie loves you when you eat your food,

And even when you are in a mood.

Your auntie loves you when you burp,

And even when you throw up on her.

Your auntie loves you when you play on the floor,

And when we go shopping and more.

Your auntie loves you when you are sick,

But remember you will always be her #1 pick.

Your auntie loves you because now she can boast,

You are one of the reasons she loves the most.

Insert baby picture here

A special note for you.

CPSIA information can be obtained
at www.ICGtesting.com
Printed in the USA
BVHW02s1430200418
513912BV00023B/281/P

9 781489 710918